Five reasons why you'll

ues, books and more...........
astic Isa

Isadora's cuddly toy, Pink Rabbit,
has been magicked to life!

ool or vampire school—
would you choose?

Isadora's family is crazy!

anting
nd black
ures

If you had to choose, would you rather be a vampire or a fairy?

I would be a fairy, because you could flutter about.
– Frankie

Fairies are better because they eat lots of fairy cakes.
– Ruby

Vampire! Because then you can stay up all night and not be told to go to bed.
– Sam

I'd like to be a vampire like Isadora's dad because they eat red food like tomatoes and strawberries.
– Harriet

I would be a vampire because they are spooky.
– Oliver

I like fairies because they are magic!
– Antonia

For vampires, fairies and humans everywhere!

And for Sarah, my glamorous mother-in-law.

OXFORD
UNIVERSITY PRESS

Great Clarendon Street, Oxford OX2 6DP

Oxford University Press is a department of the University of Oxford.
It furthers the University's objective of excellence in research, scholarship, and
education by publishing worldwide. Oxford is a registered trade mark of Oxford
University Press in the UK and in certain other countries

Copyright © Harriet Muncaster 2016
Illustrations copyright © Harriet Muncaster 2016

The moral rights of the author/illustrator have been asserted
Database right Oxford University Press (maker)

First published 2016

British Library Cataloguing in Publication Data

Data available

ISBN: 978-0-19-274431-9

1 3 5 7 9 10 8 6 4 2

Printed in Great Britain by Bell and Bain Ltd, Glasgow

Paper used in the production of this book is a natural,
recyclable product made from wood grown in sustainable forests.
The manufacturing process conforms to the environmental
regulations of the country of origin.

MIX
Paper from
responsible sources
FSC
www.fsc.org   FSC® C007785

ISADORA · MOON

Goes to School

Harriet Muncaster

OXFORD
UNIVERSITY PRESS

Chapter ONE

Isadora Moon. That's me!

Pink Rabbit and I have lots of fun together.

My mum is Countess Cordelia
Moon. She's a fairy. Yes, really!
She likes gardening, swimming in
wild streams, having magical
campfires, and sleeping outdoors
under the stars.

My dad is Count Bartholomew Moon.
He's a vampire. Yes, really! He likes
staying up all night, eating only red
food (tomatoes—yuck!), gazing at the
night sky with his special telescope,
and flying in front of a full moon.

Then there's my little sister, Baby
Honeyblossom. She's half fairy, half
vampire just like me! She likes snoozing,
gurgling, and drinking pink milk.

Pink Rabbit and I do everything together. He was my favourite stuffed toy so Mum magicked him alive.

And this is our house! That's my
bedroom at the top of the tallest turret.
I can see the whole town from my window.
Pink Rabbit is mostly not allowed to
look out of the window because he likes
jumping off things too much.

He thinks he can fly like me.

He can't fly.

Every morning I watch the human children walking down the road to school. They wear funny-looking uniforms with stripy ties.

And even though the children look very friendly . . .

And even though they look like they are having fun . . .

It makes me glad that I am a vampire fairy because vampire fairies don't have to go to school.

Or so I thought . . .

Yesterday evening I was practising my loop-the-loops out of my bedroom window when Dad called me from downstairs.

'Isadora!' he said. 'It's breakfast time!'

Dad always has his breakfast at seven o'clock at night because he sleeps during the day. Mum has hers in the morning.

This means I usually have two breakfasts. I don't mind because peanut butter on toast is my favourite thing to eat.

Dad was sitting at the table drinking a glass of his very special red smoothie juice. I think it's disgusting. I do not like red food, especially tomatoes. I know there are tomatoes in Dad's special red smoothie juice.

'One day you'll enjoy it like a proper vampire,' he says to me. 'All vampires love red food.'

But I know I won't. I'm only half vampire, after all.

Mum was there too, opening the kitchen windows to let in the fresh air, and putting bunches of flowers in vases.

We have fourteen vases of flowers in the kitchen. And a tree growing from the middle of the floor! Mum just loves to bring the outdoors inside.

Honeyblossom was grizzling in her high chair because she had dropped her bottle on the floor. I picked it up for her and filled it with some more pink milk. She hates red juice, just like me.

Dad said, 'Isadora, the time has come for you to start school.'

'But Dad,' I said. 'I am a vampire fairy. I do not need to go to school.'

'Even fairies have to go to school,' said Mum.

'Vampires too!' added Dad.

'But I don't WANT to go to school,'
I said. 'I have a perfectly busy and fine life
at home with Pink Rabbit.'

'But you might enjoy it,' insisted Dad.
'I used to love my vampire school as a
young boy.'

'And I just adored my fairy school!'
said Mum spooning some flower-nectar
yoghurt into her bowl.

'You'll have a wonderful time!' they
both smiled.

I wasn't so sure.

'But I'm not a full fairy,' I said. 'And
I'm not a full vampire. So which school
would I go to? Is there one especially for
vampire fairies? Is there a school for me?'

'Well . . . no,' said Mum. 'Not exactly.'

'You are very rare,' said Dad, sucking at his juice with a straw.

'But very special!' added Mum quickly. 'And I think fairy school would suit you marvellously.'

'But of course you may prefer vampire school,' said Dad quickly. 'It's a lot more exciting.'

'Is it?' asked Mum, sounding as though she did not agree at all. 'How about we let Isadora decide for herself.'

Pink Rabbit jumped up and down in agreement.

'Isadora can spend one day at fairy school and one night at vampire school and decide which one she likes best,' said Mum.

'But . . .' I began.

'Fantastic idea!' exclaimed Dad.

'Well . . . okay,' I said in a small voice.
I suddenly didn't fancy eating breakfast
anymore. I took Pink Rabbit's paw
and walked slowly back up the
stairs to my bedroom, thinking
very hard all the way.

'Which school would you like to go to, Pink Rabbit?' I asked. 'Vampire or fairy?'

He didn't say anything because he can't talk, but he looked up at me with his black beady eyes and gave an extra little bounce.

'A rabbit school!' I replied. 'I don't think those exist!'

When we got to my room we had a little tea party with my special bat-patterned teaset. I find having a tea party always helps me to think better. We didn't have any real tea so we put glitter in the teacups instead and Pink Rabbit got it all over his nose.

'You will have to learn to be more
civilized once we are at school,' I told him.
'I know they are very strict about manners
at vampire school.'

Pink Rabbit looked a bit ashamed so
I patted his head and brushed the glitter
off his nose.

'It doesn't matter,' I said. 'We can always go to fairy school instead. I think they are a bit more wild there.'

Pink Rabbit seemed to like that idea.

'Also,' I added, 'I bet they eat more cake at fairy school. They might even have carrot cake!'

Pink Rabbit bounced up and down with excitement. Even though he can't really eat food he likes to pretend.

Carrot cake is his favourite.

I stood up and brushed the glitter off my dress.

'Oh I just don't know!' I wailed. 'I just don't know if I am more fairy or more vampire! I love magic, sunshine, and dancing round campfires, but I also love the black of night, and flying amongst the moon and stars. It's VERY difficult. I don't know what I am or *which* school I'm going to pick!'

Pink Rabbit just shrugged and stared at me. I picked him up and we went over to my turret window. The sky twinkled all over with stars. I knew Dad would be in the second-tallest turret right now, gazing at them through his expensive astronomer's telescope.

'They are all different, you know,' I said to Pink Rabbit. 'Each one is unique. But they all look the same from down here.'

Pink Rabbit nodded wisely but I could see he had his mind on other things.

He was thinking about jumping out of the window.

I took his pink squashy paw and we stepped up onto the windowsill.

'Come on then,' I said. 'Let's go for a fly among the stars before bed.'

Chapter TWO

FAIRY SCHOOL

Teacher: Monsieur Pamplemousse

He likes: neat handwriting, butterfly spotting, camping in the wilderness, and magic.

9.00 a.m. Lesson 1—wand waving

10.30 a.m. Break time—coconut milk and organic cupcakes

11.00 a.m. Lesson 2—dancing

12.30 p.m. Lunchtime—buttercup soup with acorn pancakes

2.00 p.m. Lesson 3—flower garlands

4.00 p.m. Home time

I felt a bit nervous the night before fairy school. I think Pink Rabbit was too. I can always tell when Pink Rabbit is nervous or excited because he fidgets all night. He fidgeted all that night and I almost didn't sleep a wink.

That's why I was very tired the next day when Mum came in to get me up.

'Come on Isadora, rise and shine!' she said. 'It's time for fairy school.

I just know you're going to love it!'

She led me downstairs for my morning bath.

In the garden pond.

Mum loves to bathe in the pond among the lily pads and she thinks we should all do the same.

'It's so invigorating to be at one with nature!'

Personally I prefer when Dad is in charge of bath time. It is much less . . . *cold*. When Dad is in charge of bath time he switches all the lights off and lights lots of candles. It is very atmospheric. Sometimes he makes shadow puppets dance across the walls for me, too.

That's my favourite kind of bath time.

★ ★ ★

The fairy school was on top of a hill
covered in flowers. It looked like a giant
cupcake with windows and doors. Glitter
puffed out from the giant shiny cherry
on top.

'Doesn't it look wonderful!' said Mum.
Then she kissed my cheek and fluttered
away.

I stood looking at the school, holding Pink Rabbit's paw. He needed me to hold his paw because everything was so new and a bit scary.

My teacher was called Monsieur Pamplemousse. He had pink hair that looked like the icing on a fairy cake.

'Good morning class,' he said. 'Today
we are going to learn how to
use a magic wand!'

I had always wanted
a wand of my very own.
Suddenly I knew fairy
school was for me! After
all, who doesn't want
a glittery wand that can
grant wishes?

'We are going to make lovely things
appear,' said Monsieur Pamplemousse.
'All you need to do is wave it and *imagine*.
You should all be naturals at it!'

He handed everyone a sparkly
silver wand.

At once all the fairies began to wave their wands in the air. Nice things began to appear all over the classroom. Little kittens, giant bowls of ice cream, stripy lollipops, towering birthday cakes, freshly squeezed lemonade . . .

'What shall we wish for, Pink Rabbit?' I asked.

Pink Rabbit bounced up and down beside me.

'Carrot cake!' I said. 'What a good idea.'

I imagined a huge, towering cake covered in creamy icing and decorated with little marzipan carrots.

WHOOSH! I waved my wand.

A single carrot dropped out of the air and rolled across the floor.

I frowned. 'That was not what I was imagining,' I said.

I closed my eyes and thought of the cake again. I could see it very clearly.

I knew *exactly* what it was supposed to look like.

It had five layers and a little marzipan rabbit on the top of it.

I waved my wand again.
WHOOSH!

Still, no cake appeared. Instead, the carrot started to grow. It rolled around on the floor getting bigger and bigger all the time.

'Oh dear,' I said to Pink Rabbit.
I looked around for Monsieur
Pamplemousse but he was busy taste-
testing a fairy's cake over the other side
of the room.

The carrot was now HUGE!

'Stop growing!' I said to it. 'Stop!'

But the carrot did not stop. It kept
getting bigger and bigger and bigger.

'Monsieur Pamplemousse!' I called.
But he didn't hear me over the excited
chatter of all the fairies.

I stared at the giant carrot. A few
of the nearby fairies had noticed it now.
They were pointing and laughing.

It was embarrassing.

Quickly I pointed my wand at the carrot once more. There was a WHOOSH and a shower of sparks.

Stop growing! I thought. *Turn into a nice cake.*

The carrot stopped growing.

But it did not turn into a nice cake. Instead it sprouted a pair of black bat's wings and began to flap itself into the air.

'MONSIEUR PAMMMPLLLEEEMOOOOUUU UUSSSEEEEE!!!'

I shouted.

Finally he turned round. Just in time to see the giant carrot zooming round the classroom, crashing from wall to wall and destroying everything in its way. Cake and lemonade exploded everywhere, splattering up the walls and splashing all over the floor.

'TAKE COVER!' shouted Monsieur Pamplemousse, immediately leaping underneath his desk at the front of the class.

All the other fairies followed his lead, diving under their desks, too.

I crouched down under mine and listened to the bangs and crashes going on above my head.

43

This is all my fault! I thought, reaching out for Pink Rabbit's paw.

But Pink Rabbit's paw was not there. And nor was Pink Rabbit.

Where was he?!

I peered out from under the desk through the lemonade rain and shower of cake crumbs. My heart felt tight in my chest. What if he had been squashed?

But then I saw him! He was on the other side of the room, opening one of the big classroom windows.

What a clever rabbit! I thought.

The window swung open and a cool summery breeze floated into the room. The carrot stopped in mid-air. It did a loop-the-loop. Then it pointed its nose towards the open window and rocketed out into the sky scattering a trail of cake crumbs and lollipops behind it.

Everything went quiet for a second and no one said anything.

Then Monsieur Pamplemousse got out from under his desk and smoothed down his suit.

'Come on everyone,' he said. 'Get out from under your desks. Honestly! Fancy hiding under your desks because of a carrot!'

Then he said, 'Isadora, I'm afraid I don't think you quite have the fairy skill for wand waving.'

Oh, well, I thought. *Maybe I am completely a vampire after all.*

The next lesson was ballet.

I have taken ballet lessons since I was three so I wasn't worried about messing up this class.

We all went to change into our tutus.

I LOVE my ballet tutu. It is my second favourite thing after Pink Rabbit. It is as black as midnight with silver stars and black glitter.

It makes me feel MYSTICAL and MAGICAL.

Sometimes I wear it just for fun when I'm at home.

I put it on and then I noticed that all the other fairies were staring at me, oddly. And so was Monsieur Pamplemousse.

'You can't wear that,' they all said. 'It's black!'

'But I like black,' I said. 'Black is the colour of the sky at night. Black is a mystical and magical colour. And look how it sparkles!'

'But it's black,' said Monsieur Pamplemousse. 'We fairies wear pink ballet outfits. It's the rules.'

I was made to change out of my tutu and into a puffy pink one. It just wasn't the same.

I found I tripped up in the pink tutu. I missed my steps and I came bottom of the class. I just didn't feel like my mystical magical self.

'Oh dear,' I said to Pink Rabbit.
'I think maybe I am more vampire than
I thought.'

For lunch we had buttercup soup and
acorn pancakes.

'YUM,' said all the fairies. 'We LOVE
acorn pancakes and buttercup soup. They
taste of trees and flowers!'

I wasn't sure I wanted my food
to taste like trees and flowers but I was
very hungry so I ate it all up. It wasn't
too bad.

But nowhere near as good as peanut
butter on toast.

The last lesson of the day was flower-
garland making.

'It's almost midsummer,' said Monsieur Pamplemousse. 'A very important event in the fairy calendar. We are going to go into the magic woodland behind the school and forage for branches and flowers to make crowns! Then we will wear them next week to dance round a bonfire.'

'Ooh!' said all the fairies.

'Yes,' said Monsieur Pamplemousse. 'It is a wonderful way to be close to nature. Off we go then. Shoes off everyone!'

Everyone took off their shoes and then we all followed Monsieur Pamplemousse out of the school and to the magic woodland.

'Here we are,' he said. 'Now go and forage!'

I really wanted to do a good job after the disastrous magic wand and ballet lessons. *I'll show them,* I thought. *I'll make the best crown they've ever seen!* I began to collect up the biggest and most beautiful flowers I could find. Then I wove in some leaves and twigs. Pink Rabbit looked on in approval.

'Five minutes left!' said Monsieur Pamplemousse. 'Then I will come and look at what you've done.'

I really wanted my crown to be the best. What else could I add?

Then
I spotted some
brightly
coloured
toadstools
growing in a
ring nearby.

'These will
look like jewels!'
I said to Pink Rabbit. Quickly I picked
some and poked them into the crown.

'Beautiful! Look Pink Rabbit, I am
the queen!'

But when Monsieur Pamplemousse
saw what I had done he was not pleased
at all.

'Isadora Moon!' he said.
'You have just ruined a sacred
fairy ring!'

I blinked.

'Has no one ever told you,'
said Monsieur Pamplemousse, 'never,
ever to pick toadstools from a fairy ring?
Besides, they are poisonous toadstools.'

 I looked down at
my hands and saw that
they were covered in itchy red spots.

'Take off that crown at once! You
had better go and get some magic cream
from the school nurse,' ordered
Monsieur Pamplemousse.

Hurriedly I ripped the crown off my
head and threw it onto the ground. I felt
my eyes fill with tears.

'I didn't know,' I said. 'I didn't know
because I am not a fairy, I am a vampire!'

Then I turned round and ran back
towards the school and refused to say
another word until Mum came to pick
me up at home time.

'How was your day?' asked Mum when she saw me. 'Did you have a lovely time? Isn't fairy school just wonderful!'

And I said that no it was not wonderful at all and that actually I didn't think I was a fairy. I was just a vampire.

Mum looked a bit disappointed.

'You're probably just tired,' she said.
'I'm sure you'll feel different tomorrow.'

We went home and had breakfast
with Dad.

He was very pleased to hear that I was a vampire.

'I did think so all along,' he said as he slurped down his red juice.

After breakfast it was bed time. I was so tired after my day at fairy school that I didn't even remember to brush my teeth. I just snuggled down with Pink Rabbit under our starry quilt and fell straight asleep.

When I woke up it was morning and the sun was streaming through my turret window.

'Come on, Pink Rabbit!' I said, poking him out of bed. 'It's vampire school tonight!'

I got dressed and then we whizzed down the banister to the kitchen.

Dad was just coming in from his night-time fly. He was yawning and looking tired. Mum was busy picking apples off the tree in the kitchen. She was turning them into glasses of apple juice with her wand.

I sat down at the table and started to butter my toast.

'Are you looking forward to vampire school tonight?' asked Dad hopefully.

'Oh yes!' I said. 'I think I'm going to like vampire school.'

Dad looked pleased. He yawned and looked at the clock on the wall.

'Well then you had better go back
to bed after breakfast,' he said. 'You must
sleep all through the day so that you're nice
and fresh for the evening. Just like I do!'

I stared at him.

'But I've just got out of bed!' I said
in astonishment. 'I'm not tired!'

'Well you will be tired at school if
you don't sleep today,' said Dad. 'Come on,
finish up your toast and go up to bed.'

So I finished up my toast, but veeeery
slowly. And then I walked up the stairs to
my turret. Veeeery slowly. And then
I got back into my pyjamas veeeery
slowly and then I sat in my bed with
Pink Rabbit and stared at the sun coming

through the window.

How on earth was I supposed to get
to sleep now?

It was a very bright day and the birds
were tweeting loudly outside.

The children were being noisy too, on their way to school. After a few minutes I got up and tried to block out the light with my quilt. It didn't really work.

'MUUUM!' I shouted down the stairs.

Mum came hurrying up.

'What's the matter?' she said.

'It's too light,' I complained.

Mum magicked a dark pair of curtains across my window.

'It's too loud,' I said. 'I can hear the birds.'

Mum magicked me a pair of earplugs.

'I'm thirsty,' I said.

Mum went and fetched me a glass of apple juice.

'I think I need the bathroom.'

'Well you had better go then,' sighed Mum.

By the time it was evening I had not slept a wink. But I had drunk thirteen glasses of apple juice and been to the bathroom too many times to count.

I suddenly felt very tired. I could hardly keep my eyes open. Nor could Pink Rabbit.

'We're very sleepy,' I told Dad. 'Maybe we should just go to bed.'

'Nonsense,' said Dad. 'You've been asleep all day! Once you see how exciting vampire school is you won't want to go to bed!'

Chapter THREE

VAMPIRE SCHOOL

Teacher: Countess Darkfang

She likes: twirly handwriting, black bats, and slicked-back shiny hair.

10.00 p.m. Lesson 1—flying in formation

11.30 p.m. Break time—red juice

1.00 a.m. Lesson 2—bat training

3.00 a.m. Lunchtime—tomato soup
with tomato sandwiches and
beetroot crisps.

4.30 a.m. Lesson 3—grooming

7.00 a.m. Home time

Vampire school was also on a hill
but it was not covered with flowers
and it was not built in the shape of
a pink cupcake.

It was a tall black castle with bats
flying around its spires and turrets.
Thunder and lightning cracked through
the sky behind it.

Pink Rabbit shivered so I held his paw tight. I could tell he was a bit frightened. He doesn't like thunderstorms.

'Isn't it wonderful!' said Dad. Then he opened his black cloak and flew away into the sky, whooping with delight.

My teacher was called Countess Darkfang. She was very tall with spiky red nails.

'Good evening, class,' she said.

'Tonight we are going to learn how to fly like proper vampires. We are going to SWOOSH and GLIDE and WHIZZ across the moon! We are going to make some nice neat formation shapes in the sky. We will start with an arrow shape. A nice spiky arrow.'

Oh goody, I thought. I knew how to fly already and also I had something the other vampire children did not: wings! This would be easy.

'Follow me!' said Countess Darkfang. She lifted out her cloak and shot into the air with lightning speed.

One by one the other vampires followed. SWOOSH, GLIDE, WHIZZ.

Then it was my turn. But as I rose into
the air I realized that I wasn't swooshing or
gliding or whizzing. I was . . . flapping.

Flap flap flap went my wings. And they didn't go nearly as fast as the others. They acted more like . . . fairy wings. How had I not noticed before?

'Come on Isadora!' shouted Countess Darkfang. 'You're getting left behind!'

I flapped my wings harder, trying to keep up. I could see all the other little vampires far ahead of me, all circling round the big, bright moon.

'ARROW!' screeched Countess Darkfang.

All the other vampires arranged themselves into the shape of an arrow, leaving a space on the end for me.

'Come on Isadora!' they called.

I flapped as hard as I could and
eventually reached the space at the end
of the arrow shape. I was just getting
my breath back when Countess
Darkfang said:
'NOW ZOOM!'
Suddenly the arrow formation shot
forwards and I was left alone again in the
middle of the sky.

This was *exhausting*.

'Wait!' I cried, flapping my wings as hard as I could. 'Wait for me!'

'STOP EVERYONE!' shrieked Countess Darkfang suddenly. 'We must wait for Isadora.'

The others immediately came to a stop in the sky, still in their perfect arrow formation. Not a hair was out of place on their shiny heads.

I continued to flap along but I wasn't used to flying this fast. Now I couldn't stop! I crashed right into the vampire at the back of the arrow, my wings tangling in his cape so that we rolled into a ball and began to plummet towards the ground.

'Help!' I cried as
we spun round and
round, stars rushing
past our eyes.

'EMERGENCY!'

screeched Countess
Darkfang. She gathered
her cape and shot down towards us.
Luckily vampires are very fast flyers.
She grabbed onto my dress just before
we hit the ground.

'That was close!' she said as she set us
both upright on the ground. 'I think that's
enough flying for now.'

Pink Rabbit wiped his paw across his
forehead in relief.

'I am not sure flying is your greatest talent, Isadora,' said Countess Darkfang.

I hung my head. Maybe I *was* more fairy than vampire.

★ ★ ★

After the flying lesson it was time for a snack. Countess Darkfang gave out cartons of red juice to everyone.

'Yum!' said all the little vampires.

'Yuck!' I said. 'It's *tomato* juice!'

'Of course it is,' said Countess Darkfang. 'That's what we vampires like to drink. Delicious!'

I looked at Pink Rabbit and Pink Rabbit looked at me.

'I think,' I whispered, 'that maybe I'm not a vampire after all . . .'

Then I yawned. A big yawn.

80

I was so tired.

'Now!' said Countess

Darkfang. 'It is time for the bat-training

lesson. Follow me!'

She led us all along a dark windy

corridor to a big room where there

were hundreds, maybe *thousands* of bats

in cages.

'Bats make wonderful vampire pets,' said Countess Darkfang. 'They are especially useful for delivering post.'

She gestured around her at the bats flapping in their cages.

'You may all choose one to be your own special pet,' she said.

I looked round the room. I suddenly felt excited. I LOVE bats. We have twenty-seven of them in our attic. I liked the idea of having my own special one as a pet.

I peered into the cages. There were big bats and small bats, scrawny bats and sleek bats. Which one should I choose?

In the end
I decided on a
medium-sized one with
silky fur and beady black eyes.

'I will call him Buttons,' I said to Pink
Rabbit. 'Don't you think that's nice?'

But for some reason Pink Rabbit
did not look very happy.

'Now!' said Countess Darkfang.
'The first rule of bat training is to never
let your bat out of its cage outside or when
the window is open. Otherwise it might
fly away.'

Everyone looked round the
room to check that the turret windows
were closed.

'Of course,' continued Countess Darkfang, 'once your bat is fully trained like mine, it will never fly away.' She smiled smugly and stroked her own pet bat who was very large with fur as black as midnight.

'You may let your bat out now,' she said.

I opened the door of the little cage and Buttons flew out into the air.

'Good' said Countess Darkfang. 'Let's begin! The first thing we are going to teach our bat is how to do a somersault in the air.' She pointed at her own bat and swizzled her finger at it. Immediately the bat turned a perfect somersault.

'Now you try it,' she said to the class.

I pointed my finger at Buttons and made a circular motion. Buttons turned upside down in the air.

'Almost!' I said excitedly. 'Pink Rabbit, did you see that?'

But Pink Rabbit didn't hear me. He was busy turning perfect somersaults on the floor.

'The second thing we are going to do,' said Countess Darkfang, 'is teach our pet to sit neatly on our shoulder.' She clicked her fingers and her bat

immediately flew down onto her left
shoulder.

I clicked my finger at Buttons.

But before he had a chance to do
anything, Pink Rabbit came leaping
through the air and landed on my
shoulder with a thump.

'Hey!' I said. 'Pink Rabbit, you have
to get down!'

But Pink Rabbit did not want to get
down. He held onto my neck with his pink
paws and dug his soft feet firmly into my
collarbone.

'Really,' I said. 'You do, or we'll get into trouble.' I picked him off me and set him on the floor.

I turned my attention back to Buttons and clicked my fingers at him again.

'Come on,' I urged him.

But Buttons didn't seem very interested in coming to sit on my shoulder. He was suddenly fascinated with something over the other side of the room. What was it? I turned to see and then gasped.

The turret window! It was swinging wide open!

Oh NO! I thought as the air suddenly became full of the sound of flapping wings.

All the pet bats, including Buttons, started to dash towards the open window.

WHOOSH! They went. FLAP! SWISH! FREEDOM!

'ARGHHH!' screeched Countess Darkfang. 'WHO HAS OPENED THE WINDOW?' She lifted her cape and leapt across the room to close it.

But it was too late.

The bats were gone.

I glanced across at Pink Rabbit. He was loitering by the open window looking very pleased with himself.

'Isadora Moon!' Countess Darkfang shouted. 'That Pink Rabbit of yours is a LIABILITY. A NUISANCE! I am hereby BANNING him from vampire school!'

'But . . .' I said.

'No buts,' said Countess Darkfang. 'After today he is never EVER allowed back.'

Then she picked up her cape and swished out of the room to the lunch hall.

I thought Pink Rabbit didn't look sorry at all.

After lunch, which was more red food (tomato sandwiches and tomato soup with beetroot crisps—yuck!) it was time for the last lesson of the day. Grooming.

'Grooming is VERY important,' said Countess Darkfang as she walked round the classroom handing out little silver hand mirrors, spiky hairbrushes and pots of gloopy hair gel. 'Vampires must look their best. Shiny, neat hair is extremely important. It's the rules.'

She patted her own perfect hair proudly. There was so much gel in it that it made a 'tap tap' sound when she touched it.

All the other vampires began to comb their already neat and shiny hair, smiling as they did so.

I picked up the hairbrush. This was not going to be easy. My hair is quite . . . wild.

I put the hairbrush to my head.

A minute later it was stuck!

'Countess Darkfang,' I called. 'The hairbrush is stuck in my hair!'

Countess Darkfang came hurrying over, tutting loudly. She gave the hairbrush a little pull but it didn't budge.

'Your hair is just too knotty,' she complained. She yanked a little harder.

'Ouch!' I said.

And then a bit harder . . .

'OUCH!' I yelled.

At last the hairbrush came out.

And so did a big clump of my hair.

'Let's try the gel instead,' said
Countess Darkfang. She scooped a big
handful out from the pot and began to
smooth it over my head.

'This'll do it,' she said.

But the gel did not do it. My hair would just not stay down. I peered into the hand mirror and watched as Countess Darkfang tried to flatten it. Every time she tried to smooth a piece of hair into place it would ping right back up again.

Ping, ping, PING!

'Hmm,' frowned Countess Darkfang. 'Isadora, your hair is WILD!'

I smiled sleepily. I don't mind my hair being wild. In fact, I quite like it. I closed my eyes as Countess Darkfang continued to cover my head with handfuls of the gloopy gel. It felt quite soothing. And I was so sleepy . . .

'I WILL tame it,' I heard her say as I drifted off. 'I WILL! This is not satisfactory . . .'

And then before I knew it I was fast asleep.

Dad was not very impressed when he came to pick me up at the end of the night.

'You're not supposed to fall asleep at vampire school Isadora!' he said.

'I know,' I said sadly. 'I think maybe I'm not a vampire at all.'

Dad looked disappointed.

'I expect you'll feel differently after you've had a good sleep,' he said hopefully. 'Let's go home.'

So we flew home together and I went straight to bed like Dad does every morning.

And I slept through the whole morning and didn't wake up until three o'clock!

It felt very strange. When I got up Mum was waiting for me in the kitchen. She had made me a sandwich. I could tell she had used magic to make it because every time I bit into it the flavour of it changed. First it was ham, then peanut butter, then cucumber, then . . .

'YUCK! Tomatoes!' I yelled.

Sometimes Mum's shortcuts don't pay off.

'Oh dear,' she said. 'Sorry. I still haven't got that spell quite right. Let me try again.'

'It's okay,' I said. 'I'm not hungry anymore.'

'So, how was vampire school?' Mum asked. 'Did you like it better than fairy school?'

'I'm not sure . . .' I said. 'I still don't know if I am more fairy or vampire.'

'Oh,' said Mum. 'I see.'

I took a handful of cereal and wandered into the garden with Pink Rabbit. We could see the school children walking home along the pavement through the fence. Some of them were scruffy and some of them were neat. Some of them were loud and some of them were quiet. Some of them were tall and some of them were short. Some of them were fat and some of them were thin. And some of them were just in between.

And the thing was, none of them seemed to mind!

I suddenly remembered what Dad had told me about the stars in the sky.

How every one of them is different, but
how they are all just as beautiful and
I thought, *Maybe it doesn't matter if
I am a little different. Different can be
beautiful, too.*

I pressed my face closer to the fence
and one of the children saw me. He had
blonde hair and lots of freckles and a big
smile.

He said, 'Hey you, what's your name?'

I didn't say anything because I suddenly felt very shy.

But the boy didn't leave. He came over to where I was and gazed up at my house.

'Cool house!' he said.

Then he spotted my wings. 'Cool wings!' he said. 'Can you really fly with them?'

I nodded and fluttered a few inches off the ground.

'Awesommme!' shouted the boy.

Some of the other children were coming over now.

'WOW!' they said. 'We've always wanted to talk to you!'

'Really?' I said in astonishment.

'Oh, yes,' said the boy. 'We walk past your house every day on our way to school. We've seen you up in that turret window.'

'*And* we've seen a fairy here!' said
a little girl with pigtails who was busy
munching on a peanut butter sandwich.
'A fairy with pink hair! Me and my friends
are always trying to peek in to see her.'

'Oh that's just my mum,' I said.

'Some of us have seen a vampire,'
shuddered the boy. 'A really scary vampire
with a black cape and pointy teeth. Some
kids in our class are too scared to walk
past your house, you know.' He puffed out
his chest. 'Not me!'

I laughed.

'That's just my dad,' I said. 'He's not
scary at all!'

'So there really are fairies and

vampires living here?' the children asked.
'Really?'

'Yes!' I said. 'Really! And there is also
a vampire fairy living here . . . ME!'

'A vampire fairy!' said the children.
'That's even better!'

'I wish *I* was a vampire fairy,'
said a girl with pink plastic clips in her
curly hair.

Suddenly I felt very proud to be me.

'My name is Isadora,' I told the
children.

'That's a nice name,' said the curly-
haired girl. 'My name is Zoe and that's

Sashi.' She pointed to the girl with pigtails.

'And I'm Bruno,' said the boy. 'So what school do you go to? Is it a special school for vampire fairies?'

'Well,' I began, 'I . . .'

But just then I heard a sound from the house.

'ISADOOOORA!'

It was Mum calling me inside.

'I have to go,' I said to the children.
'But it was really nice to meet you! Maybe
we can chat through the fence again
one day? I can bring us peanut butter
sandwiches!'

'Oh yes!' said all the children. 'Please
come back! We can have a picnic. And
bring your pink rabbit again too, he's so
funny!'

'Peanut butter sandwiches are my
favourite,' said Sashi.

'Mine too!' I said. 'I like them with
apple juice.'

'That sounds tasty!' said Bruno.

'ISADOOOORA! What are you doing?' called Mum again.

'I really have to go!' I said.

I said goodbye to the children and ran back to the house with Pink Rabbit bouncing joyfully along behind me.

My run turned into a skip and then a skippity-hop. I couldn't help it.

I suddenly felt so happy.

'There you are,' said Mum when I got inside.

'Oh good,' yawned Dad. It was still a bit early for him to be awake so he was wearing his sunglasses.

'We have decided to see if you can go to *both* schools,' Mum said. 'It's the perfect solution!'

'But . . .' I said.

'You can go to fairy school in the morning, come home for a quick nap, and then go to vampire school in the evening,' she said.

'But . . .' I said, 'I don't *want* to do that.'

Mum looked surprised. 'Why ever not?' she said.

'I've thought of a much better solution . . . I want to go to REGULAR HUMAN SCHOOL!'

Mum and Dad both gasped.

'Oh no no NO!' they exclaimed. 'Why on earth would you want to go there? You are magical! You are special! You need to go to a special school. It's vampire school or fairy school.'

I shook my head.

'No,' I said. 'I want to go to regular school.'

'But it's full of humans!' said Dad, astonished. 'Humans are *so* weird. They hardly get any fresh air. They sit around watching boxes all day. They eat beige food and they use screens to talk to each other . . .'

'They can't even fly!' added Mum.

'Well, I just spoke to some of the children and they were very nice. There was one called Bruno and one called Zoe and one called—'

'You *spoke* to them!' gasped Dad in horror.

'But . . . but . . . they're not like you,' said Mum. 'You are different.'

'I know,' I said. 'But they were

all different too. Like the stars that Dad looks at through his telescope. And they didn't mind that I am not a full vampire or a full fairy. In fact they thought it was *interesting.*'

'Hmm . . .' said Dad. 'Humans are very odd.'

'Well, I like them,' I said. 'I'm starting to think that it's *you* two who are a little strange!'

'Well!' said Mum, tapping the apple tree with her wand so that it started to grow oranges instead.

'Really!' said Dad, pushing his sunglasses further up his nose.

'Yes,' I told them. 'But you know, I think that's a good thing. Things would be very boring otherwise.'

Pink Rabbit nodded wisely beside me.

'And so,' I continued firmly, 'I have decided that regular school is the perfect place for me!'

'Hmm,' said Mum, picking an orange off the tree.

'Are you *sure* you wouldn't rather go to vampire school?' Dad asked.

'I am sure,' I told him.

'And *sure* you wouldn't rather go to fairy school?' added Mum.

'Yes!' I said.

'Well then,' said Dad. 'Maybe regular school *is* the place for you.'

'Maybe it *could* be the perfect place for you,' said Mum, holding her arms out to me for a hug.

I smiled and Pink Rabbit bounced up and down beside me.

'I know it is!' I told them happily. 'Human school is the perfect place for a vampire fairy like me!'

Harriet Muncaster, that's me! I'm the
author and illustrator of Isadora Moon.
Yes really! I love anything teeny tiny,
anything starry, and everything glittery.

stories have you read?

Love Isadora Moon?
Why not try these too . . .